D0776877

A Note to Parents and Caregivers:

Read-it! Readers are for children who are just starting on the amazing road to reading. These beautiful books support both the acquisition of reading skills and the love of books.

 The PURPLE LEVEL presents basic topics and objects using high frequency words and simple language patterns.

 The RED LEVEL presents familiar topics using common words and repeating sentence patterns.

 The BLUE LEVEL presents new ideas using a larger vocabulary and varied sentence structure.

 The YELLOW LEVEL presents more challenging ideas, a broad vocabulary, and wide variety in sentence structure.

 The GREEN LEVEL presents more complex ideas, an extended vocabulary range, and expanded language structures.

 The ORANGE LEVEL presents a wide range of ideas and concepts using challenging vocabulary and complex language structures.

When sharing a book with your child, read in short stretches, pausing often to talk about the pictures. Have your child turn the pages and point to the pictures and familiar words. And be sure to reread favorite stories or parts of stories.

There is no right or wrong way to share books with children. Find time to read with your child, and pass on the legacy of literacy.

Adria F. Klein, Ph.D.
Professor Emeritus
California State University
San Bernardino, California

Editor: Jill Kalz
Designer: Amy Muehlenhardt
Page Production: Brandie Shoemaker
Art Director: Nathan Gassman
Associate Managing Editor: Christianne Jones
The illustrations in this book were created with watercolor and pencil.

Picture Window Books
5115 Excelsior Boulevard
Suite 232
Minneapolis, MN 55416
877-845-8392
www.picturewindowbooks.com

Printed in the United States of America.

Library of Congress Cataloging-in-Publication Data
Klein, Adria F. (Adria Fay), 1947–
Max's fun day / by Adria F. Klein ; illustrated by Mernie Gallagher-Cole.
p. cm. — (Read-it! readers. The life of Max)
Summary: Max and his good friend Don, who is in a wheelchair, have a lot of fun
together, whether they are at the park, in the library, or at a restaurant.
ISBN-13: 978-1-4048-3150-6 (library binding)
ISBN-10: 1-4048-3150-9 (library binding)
ISBN-13: 978-1-4048-3549-8 (paperback)
ISBN-10: 1-4048-3549-0 (paperback)
[1. Friendship—Fiction. 2. Hispanic Americans—Fiction. 3. African Americans—
Fiction. 4. People with disabilities—Fiction.] I. Gallagher-Cole, Mernie, ill. II. Title.
PZ7.K678324Maym 2006
[E]—dc22   2006027291

Max's Fun Day

by Adria F. Klein
illustrated by Mernie Gallagher-Cole

Special thanks to our advisers for their expertise:

Adria F. Klein, Ph.D.
Professor Emeritus, California State University
San Bernardino, California

Susan Kesselring, M.A.
Literacy Educator
Rosemount–Apple Valley–Eagan (Minnesota) School District

PiCTURE WiNDOW BOOKS
Minneapolis, Minnesota

Max and Don are good friends.

They go to a lot of places together.

Max and Don go to the petting zoo
with Max's mom.

They feed the baby ducks.

They pet the goats and lambs.

Max and Don go to the library.

13

They listen to the librarian read a story about the ocean.

They like learning about whales, sharks, and dolphins.

Max and Don go to dinner
with Don's parents.

17

Max eats a hamburger.

Don eats macaroni and cheese.

Max and Don both want dessert.

They both ask for ice cream.

Max and Don go to a lot of places together. Max and Don are good friends.

More *Read-it!* Readers

Bright pictures and fun stories help you practice your reading skills. Look for more books at your level.

Max and the Adoption Day Party
Max Celebrates Chinese New Year
Max Goes to a Cookout
Max Learns Sign Language
Max Stays Overnight

Max Goes on the Bus
Max Goes Shopping
Max Goes to School
Max Goes to the Barber
Max Goes to the Dentist
Max Goes to the Library

Looking for a specific title or level? A complete list of *Read-it!* Readers is available on our Web site:
www.picturewindowbooks.com